This book
belongs to

....

....

EGMONT

We bring stories to life

Special thanks to Ian McCue and Micaela Winter
Special thanks also to Dr Deborah Weber
Written by Katrina Pallant and Nancy Parent
Illustrated by Valeria Orlando and Fabio Paciulli, Tomatofarm

First published in Great Britain 2018 by Egmont UK Limited,
The Yellow Building, 1 Nicholas Road, London W11 4AN

 Thomas the Tank Engine & Friends™

HiT entertainment **CREATED BY BRITT ALLCROFT**

Based on The Railway Series by The Reverend W Awdry
© 2018 Gullane (Thomas) LLC. Thomas the Tank Engine & Friends and
Thomas & Friends are trademarks of Gullane (Thomas) Limited.

© 2018 HIT Entertainment Limited.

ISBN 978 1 4052 8907 8

68003/1

Printed in EU

DELIVERY AT THE DOCKS

A story about making friends

It was going to be a very busy day at Brendam Docks on the Island of Sodor. The Fat Controller told Thomas, Percy and Salty about a new arrival.

"Good morning, Engines. Today we have a special job to do, and Frankie is coming from the Mainland to help us. We need to unload all of the cargo from the ferry by three o'clock, so you should all work together to get the job done quickly."

Meanwhile, on the ship Frankie was excited to be going to Sodor. She was looking forward to seeing her friend Thomas again.

"I hope the other engines like me," she said. "It can be a bit scary to meet new engines, but I love making friends!"

Thomas and Percy watched as Cranky lowered Frankie to the ground.

"Hi, Frankie," Thomas said cheerily. "Welcome to Sodor!"

But Frankie was too nervous to answer. "Please don't drop me!" she said to Cranky. "This isn't how we'd lower an engine at the Steelworks."

"Excuse *me*!" snapped Cranky. "I do know how to lift and load. It's my job."

Percy looked a little worried. "I hope we can all get along," he whispered to Thomas.

"Don't worry, Percy," Thomas said. "Frankie will fit right in."

Percy was just about to start pulling the flatbeds of cargo when Frankie stopped him. "It would be much quicker for me to shunt these," she said helpfully. "That's how we sort trucks at the Steelworks."

Percy looked confused. "But we're not *at* the Steelworks," he said. "And it's supposed to be my job to move the trucks."

Salty decided to tell one of his tall tales. "Listen up, me hearties," he began.

But Frankie interrupted him. "We don't tell stories while we're working at the Steelworks. It's quicker to do our work first."

Salty was shocked. "This is Brendam Docks, and here we like to do things *our* way."

Thomas was sad to find his friends looking so upset, and Frankie looking worried.

"Your friends don't seem to like me very much," Frankie said.

"Don't worry," said Thomas. "Sometimes, being a good friend is learning how others do things, and what to do to show that you care."

Soon another ship arrived at the Docks.
The cranes, engines and shunters all
wanted to be Really Useful. So they
got busy unloading the ferry.

As Thomas chuffed in with another freight car, he saw Cranky unloading a stack of crates.

"Hey, Frankie!" Cranky called. "Watch how we do things at the Docks."

Cranky was so busy showing off to Frankie, he didn't see that his crates were about to go flying into Percy's flatbeds.

"Percy, quick!" cried Thomas. "Move those trucks out of the way!"

Percy peeped and puffed so fast and hard that he crashed into Cranky's crates and they spilled steel pipes onto the Dock. Hurrying over to help, Salty smashed right into Thomas.

"Bust my buffers!" cried Thomas. "Now what do we do?"

"Oh no!" Salty cried. "The ferry leaves at three o'clock, and we haven't finished unloading the cargo."

Frankie wanted to help and quickly started to shunt the steel pipes out of the way. "Don't worry. I'll move the pipes!" she said.

"Well done, Frankie," Thomas said.
"If we all work together, we can
get the job done."

Frankie could see that everyone was still upset so she asked Salty to tell a story.

Salty looked surprised. "I thought you didn't tell stories at the Steelworks."

"But we're not *at* the Steelworks," she said.

Everyone laughed. While they all cleaned up the Docks, Salty told his story.

By three o'clock, the work was done and the ferry could leave on time. The Fat Controller arrived, and everyone wanted to tell him how Frankie had helped save the day.

"I'm glad to hear that Frankie has been Really Useful," he said.

"And she has become our new friend," said Salty.

Frankie smiled at everyone. "I'm so glad we could all work together."

Thomas, Percy, Salty, and Cranky knew they couldn't have done the job without their new friend.

"Welcome to the team, Frankie!" said Thomas.

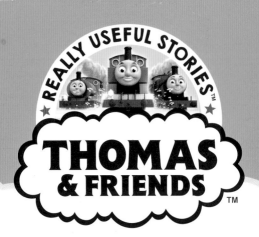

THOMAS & FRIENDS™

REALLY USEFUL STORIES™

Really Useful Stories™ can help children talk about new experiences. Here are some questions about this story that can help you talk about making friends.

Who did The Fat Controller bring to Sodor to help out at the Docks?

What did Frankie do to upset Cranky, Percy and Salty?

What did Thomas tell Frankie when she was worried that no one liked her?

How did being friends help the engines to solve their problem?